Katie Woo,
Where Are You?

by Fran Manushkin

illustrated by Tammie Lyon

PICTURE WINDOW BOOKS
a capstone imprint

Katie Woo is published by Picture Window Books
a Capstone imprint
1710 Roe Crest Drive
North Mankato, Minnesota 56003
www.capstonepub.com

Text © 2012 Fran Manushkin
Illustrations © 2012 Picture Window Books

Library of Congress Cataloging-in-Publication Data
Manushkin, Fran.
  Katie Woo, where are you? / by Fran Manushkin; illustrated by Tammie Lyon.
      p. cm. — (Katie Woo)
  Summary: While shopping with her parents in a mall, Katie helps a lost boy, not realizing that she may be lost, too.
ISBN 978-1-4048-6517-4 (library binding)
ISBN 978-1-4048-6853-3 (pbk.)
  [1. Lost children—Fiction. 2. Shopping—Fiction. 3. Chinese Americans—Fiction.] I. Lyon, Tammie, ill. II. Title.
  PZ7.M3195Kbm 2011
  [E]—dc22   2011005490

Art Director: Kay Fraser
Graphic Designer: Emily Harris

Printed in the United States of America in Stevens Point, Wisconsin.
122014
008671R

Table of Contents

Chapter 1
A Trip to the Mall 5

Chapter 2
Where's Katie?............................12

Chapter 3
A Happy Ending............................22

Chapter 1
A Trip to the Mall

Katie Woo was watching

a TV show about a lost baby

whale. Suddenly, the picture

went out!

Her dad tried to fix it. "It's

too old," he said. "We need a

new TV."

"I need a party dress,"
said Katie's mom. "Let's go to
the mall."

"I guess I'll never know if
the whale mom found her
baby," Katie sighed.

The mall
was only ten
minutes away.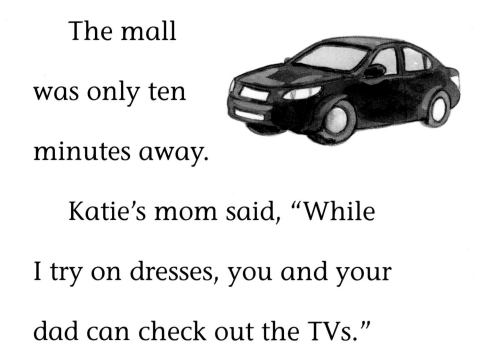

Katie's mom said, "While
I try on dresses, you and your
dad can check out the TVs."

Katie walked in front
of her dad. Suddenly he
stopped and said, "Look at
these neat lawn mowers!"

But Katie didn't hear him.
Someone was talking on the
loud speaker.

"We are looking

for a lost boy," said

the speaker. "He

has blond hair and

is wearing a red T-shirt. His

name is Teddy. If you find

him, bring him to the Lost

and Found."

"Poor Teddy," said Katie.

"It's awful to be lost."

Katie did not notice that her dad was gone. She was looking at the TVs. They all showed the end of Katie's program about the whale.

"Hurray!" Katie said. "His

mom found him! I hope

someone finds Teddy."

Chapter 2

Where's Katie?

"I'd like to be a TV star,"

Katie decided.

She put

on sunglasses,

a pretty scarf,

and a big, floppy hat.

Katie walked past her

dad. He did not know it was

her under the fancy glasses,

scarf, and hat.

Katie did not see her dad,

either.

Katie walked past her
mom, trying on a dress. They
did not notice each other.

"I look awesome!" said
Katie, looking into a mirror.

"I look awful," said her

mother, looking into a

mirror, too.

Katie passed a blond

boy in a red T-shirt. He was

crying.

She stopped and asked,

"Is your name Teddy?"

"Yes," he sniffled.

"Yay!" Katie said. "I found

the lost boy."

At that same moment,

Katie's mom asked her dad,

"Where's Katie?"

"Oh, no!" said her dad. "I

thought she was with you."

Katie found the Lost and
Found. "Here's Teddy," she
said proudly. "I found him."

"Good for you," said the
lady. "But now somebody
else is lost."

She said on the loud speaker, "We are looking for a lost girl. She has dark hair and her name is Katie Woo. If you find her, bring her to the Lost and Found."

Katie laughed. "I'm not lost!" she said. "I'm right here!"

Chapter 3
A Happy Ending

Katie's parents were so

happy to see her!

"Guess what?" Katie told them. "The baby whale's mom found her too! And I found Teddy."

"I love happy endings," said her mom.

"But we still have to get the TV and the dress," said Katie's dad.

"I'll lead the way," Katie offered. "I know where everything is."

And this time, nobody got lost.

About the Author

Fran Manushkin is the author of many popular picture books, including *How Mama Brought the Spring; Baby, Come Out!; Latkes and Applesauce: A Hanukkah Story;* and *The Tushy Book*. There is a real Katie Woo — she's Fran's great-niece — but she never gets in half the trouble of the Katie Woo in the books. Fran writes on her beloved Mac computer in New York City, without the help of her two naughty cats, Miss Chippie and Goldy.

About the Illustrator

Tammie Lyon began her love for drawing at a young age while sitting at the kitchen table with her dad. She continued her love of art and eventually attended the Columbus College of Art and Design, where she earned a bachelors degree in fine art. After a brief career as a professional ballet dancer, she decided to devote herself full time to illustration. Today she lives with her husband, Lee, in Cincinnati, Ohio. Her dogs, Gus and Dudley, keep her company as she works in her studio.